This book belongs to:

_____

_____

_____

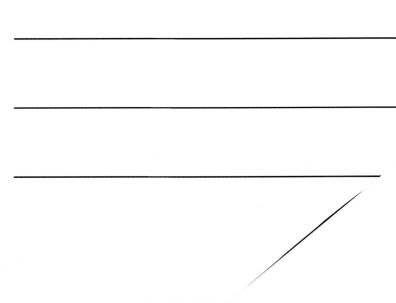

For Tom, Rosie, Raife, Monty
and Dr Jennifer Pinney

# Delivery Dog
## and the masks

*Sara Beels*

Bumblebee Books
*London*

"Morning Dan! What have we got on today?"
"Jump in the van, I'll explain on the way!"

"Whenever I look, there's more and more.
Please can you tell me what these masks are for?"

*"Do I put this paper mask on my bum?*
*Don't tell me, I know it goes on my tum!"*

"You funny dog! Those aren't the places,
People use them to cover their faces."

*"Why do I need to do that too?"*

"Delivery Dog, masks aren't for you!"

"When people are ill they can cough and sneeze,
The virus moves in the air, it's a disease."

*"These masks are very important to wear,
So I must help because I really care.
Hospital is the place for when you're sick.
I may be small but I can get there quick!"*

"*Stop Dan, stop! Its the school, we're here!*"
"We've got masks for you! Some fabric, some clear."

"I bet the children are missing their mates."

"Not long now until we open the gates."

"We need the new masks, right away.
With your help, Dog, the kids can play!"

"There's lots of boxes, this is a big task!
Look! There's a little girl, with a mask.

She's stood in a long queue, in her pink shoes.
I think those people must have read the news.

Let's get it done, Dan, there's no time to stop,
They need these masks to open the shop!"

"Out to the countryside, on to the farm.
We need to keep the farmers safe from harm."

"The hairdresser's is open for a cut.
We're really pleased it's no longer shut."

*"It's pouring with rain, now we're at the vets.*
*This is the place for sick and poorly pets.*
*I am a bit scared Dan. Can we hurry?"*

"It's okay Dog, all fine, don't worry."

"This vet is helping pets to get better."

*"Can we go now? I'm just getting wetter!
Last year being at the vets made me cry."*

"It was very important to look at your eye."

*"The vet gave my eyes a special test.
I lay on a blanket for a rest.
On this side of my face, I can't see.
Don't worry, I'm just happy being me!"*

*"All this hard work has put me in the mood*
*For a gigantic, tasty bowl of food.*
*Is it time to go home and play now Dan?"*

"Yes! Let's park the big delivery van."

Dan washes his hands now the day is done.
Delivery Dog wants to have some fun!

"Come on now Dan, it's time for a walk.
Just think, some people say that dogs can't talk!"

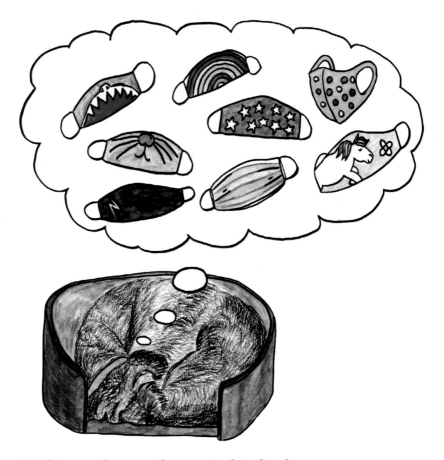

Delivery dog curls up, in his bed.
Magical masks go around in his head...

See how many masks you can spot when you're out for a walk.
Tick off these masks in your Mask Spotter's guide:-

Magical masks ☐ 

Black masks ☐ 

Spotty masks ☐ 

Unicorn masks ☐ 

Animal masks ☐ 

Starry masks ☐ 

Blue paper masks ☐ 

Visors ☐ 

BUMBLEBEE PAPERBACK EDITION

A CIP catalogue record for this title is
available from the British Library.

ISBN: 978-1-83934-360-5

Bumblebee Books is an imprint of
Olympia Publishers.

First Published in 2021

Bumblebee Books
Tallis House
2 Tallis Street
London
EC4Y 0AB

Printed in Great Britain

www.olympiapublishers.com

## About the Author

Sara spent nine years as an early years teacher both in the North East and the South West of England. Now a mum of two children under four, she understands first-hand the challenges that this pandemic has brought parents as they try to make sense of our changing world. Sara knows from her work with young children that the best thing that we can do, is to take time to really listen to what they have to say, because it is being listened to that will make the biggest difference to their mental health in the future.